The Fable

written by Sarah Philpot

illustrated by Sarah Gledhill

atmosphere press

To my incredibly talented family.
Chase the lion.

Once upon a time in a small country town,
lived a funny old man who always wore a frown.

He taught all the children how to fish for trout down by the pond where the cattails sprout.

Though shy and timid most of the time,
he told witty stories with excitement and rhyme.

His stories taught lessons and cheered people up.
He gave them hope, love, and all things that build up.

Since his stories brought joy to everyone in town,
no one understood why he always wore a frown.

One day a little boy watched the man with awe,
as he told his wild stories without a single flaw.

The boy bravely asked the man why he seemed so sad,
for it made no sense at all with the talent that he had.

The man felt ashamed and looked down at his feet.
"I'm not good at anything," he answered in defeat.

Then he confessed, "I can't read, spell, or write,
because words float around and won't stay in sight."

"The doctor called it dyslexia, I think.
It makes me feel foolish, and I just want to shrink."

The boy jumped up and threw his hands in the air.
"Mister, you're not foolish," the little boy declared.

"We each have weaknesses we wish we could hide,
but we also have st-strengths resting inside."

"I have a stutter that makes it hard to sp-speak.
I also have strengths that make me unique."

From a bag on his back he pulled out a sketchbook.
He laid it on the ground and said, "Come ta-take a look."

Each page held a painting of beautiful art,
all created by the boy straight from his heart.

"I g-give my paintings away to bring others joy.
It's how I share my g-gift with the world," said the boy.

"This stutter won't k-keep me from my calling,
since I share joy with others through my dr-drawings."

"Although you struggle with the wr-written word,
imagine if your s-stories had never been heard."

"Anyone can tell stories," the old man replied,
as he tipped up his hat and made it cockeyed.

The boy took the man's hand and said with care,
"Your stories g-give a hope and joy that are rare."

"The people around here c-call you the Fable King,
for we love your st-stories and the lessons they bring."

Then the boy grabbed a painting from his pack.
He showed it to the man, and his jaw went slack.

To the man's surprise it was a painting of him,
telling his stories from a fallen tree limb.

The faces in the painting were all cheerful with glee, gazing in simple wonder as he told his stories.

He never noticed he had an impact before,
but this painting now made it hard to ignore.

A happy little tear ran down the man's cheek
as he realized he was special and truly unique.

Then, like a shining light, a miracle occurred,
the man began to smile as his heart was stirred.

"No more frowning for me," he told the boy.
"My purpose is clear: I am meant to bring joy."

"I may not be able to read very well,
but I have plenty of stories still left to tell."

From that day forward the man beamed with pride.
He was confident, hopeful, and happy inside.

About the Author

Sarah Philpot is an Oklahoma Public
School teacher who has a passion
to help students and adults
recognize their God-given talents
and pursue their callings despite
any setbacks they may have.

About the Illustrator

Sarah Gledhill lives in Lancashire, United Kingdom. Having
spent decades bouncing around the hot, dry African veld in
a Landi, sharing life and adventures with four sons and a
wonderful variety of animals, she is now happily rediscov-
ering the hedgerows, woodlands, waterways and dry stone
walls of the UK.

About Atmosphere Press

Atmosphere Press is an independent, full-service publisher for excellent books in all genres and for all audiences. Learn more about what we do at atmospherepress.com.

We encourage you to check out some of Atmosphere's latest children's book releases, which are available online and via order from your local bookstore:

The King's Drapes, a picture book by Jocelyn Tambascio
You are the Moon, a picture book by Shana Rachel Diot
Onionhead, a picture book by Gary Ziskovsky
Odo and the Stranger, a picture book by Mark Johnson
Jack and the Lean Stalk, a picture book by Raven Howell
Brave Little Donkey, a picture book by Rachel L. Pieper
Buried Treasure, a picture book by Anne Krebbs
Young Yogi and the Mind Monsters, by Sonja Radvila
Bello the Cello, a picture book by Dennis Mathew

CPSIA information can be obtained
at www.ICGtesting.com
Printed in the USA
BVHW022048250221
600911BV00023B/912